For M, just because.
Meg McKinlay

To my dearest Drea and my little River — I am at home when I am with you. Love always.
Andrew Frazer

First published 2017 by FREMANTLE PRESS
25 Quarry Street, Fremantle WA 6160
www.fremantlepress.com.au

Printed by Everbest Printing Company, China.

National Library of Australia
Cataloguing-in-Publication entry available
ISBN 9781925164848

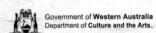

Government of **Western Australia**
Department of **Culture and the Arts.**

Fremantle Press is supported by the State Government through the Department of Culture and the Arts.

DRAWN ONWARD

MEG McKINLAY & ANDREW FRAZER

FREMANTLE PRESS

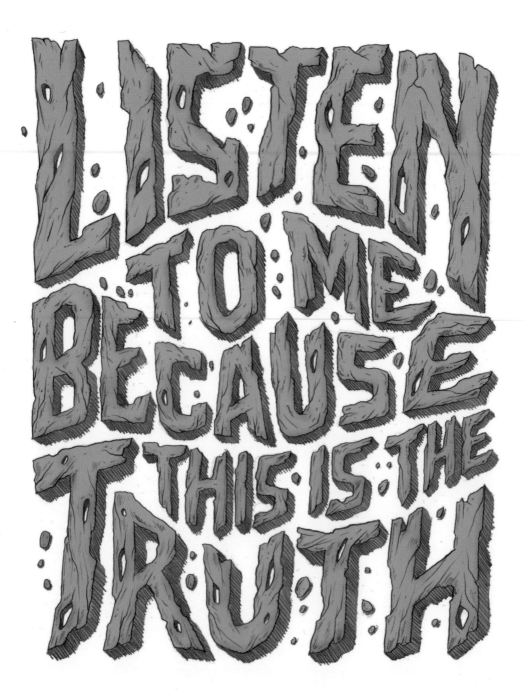

I HOPE YOU KNOW THAT THE WORLD WILL ALWAYS BE GLOOMY AND DARK

THERE IS NO LIGHT ON THE MORRISON & IT IS FOOLISH TO THINK YOU CAN CHANGE ANYTHING AT ALL

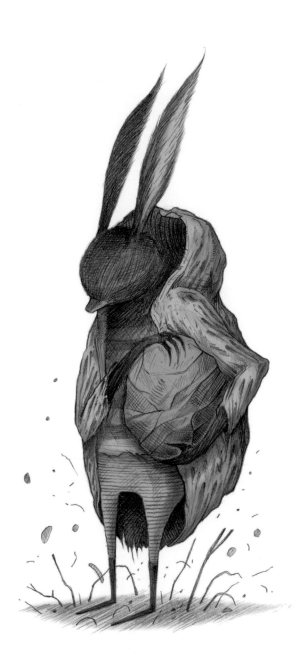

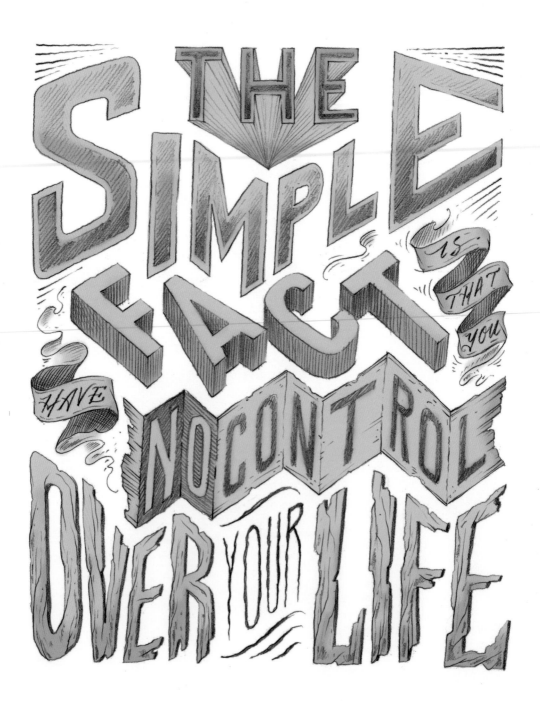

YOU ARE SOMEONE WHO CAN'T HOPE TO DO ANYTHING AT ALL JUST A TINY SPECK TOSSED THIS WAY & THAT

PEOPLE WHO THINK THEY ARE IMPORTANT & PRECIOUS ARE WRONG

YOU NEED TO SEE
THESE THINGS:
WAKE UP NOW
BEFORE
IT'S TOO LATE!

NOW
Before IT'S TOO LATE
WAKE UP!
YOU NEED to SEE
These Things Are
WRONG

IMPORTANT & PRECIOUS

PEOPLE THINK WHO THEY ARE JUST A Tiny Speck TOSSED THIS WAY & THAT CAN'T HOPE TO DO ANYTHING AT ALL

IMAGINE

WHY WOULD YOU

Nothing Good

IS AROUND THE CORNER

& YOU HAVE NO CONTROL OVER

Your Life?

IT IS FOOLISH to THINK · THERE is NO Light on the Horizon & the WORLD WILL ALWAYS BE GLOOMY ‹AND› DARK I Hope YOU KNOW THAT